HOW I MADE IT OVER

PAMELA ROUSE

SHAR-SHEY PUBLISHING COMPANY LLC

Copyright © 2020 Pamela Rouse

ISBN: 13: 978-0-9997922-2-3

Publisher: Shar- Shey Publishing Company LLC

Book Cover Designed by: Dynasty's Visionary Designs

Edited by: Angela McClain

Shar-Shey Publishing, LLC

P.O. Box 402

Swiftwater, PA 18370

(973) 348-5067

sspublishingcompany@gmail.com

www.sharsheypublishingcompany.com

I dedicate this book to my loving mother Nazelean Baccus, who has gone on to be with My Lord and Savior. To my father, Henry Baccus, who is still here, thank you for believing in me. To my children, Norrita, Ronald, and Ayisha, I thank you for making this book possibly, by giving me nine and a half wise grandchildren: number ten is still in the mommy oven. To my husband, Howard Rouse, thank you for always helping around the house when I was writing and when I wasn't writing...Laugh Out Loud, thanks hunny.

CONTENTS

My Prayer

Father God, I need Your help in writing this book. Lord I need Your Holy Spirit to take over my mind, that my book will cause life changing experiences to all those who would read my story. Take it out of the natural and let them read it in Your spirit so that my story may give them Your insight with wisdom, understanding, and clarity. In the name of Jesus, I pray: Amen.

Introduction

How I Made It Over is a book that will inspire many people's lives. My book is about me and my family, but most of all, it is my trust in Jesus. Life has its ups and downs, but with Jesus, all things are possible. I've come a long way on this journey with Jesus, and I wouldn't change my life experiences or any of my encounters with all my children and grandkids. They have made me and my family who we are today. In life, we find things aren't always good, but we make the best out of it. We find that, as we grow older, the more aware we become of the things that are most important to us —family. It has been a rough road for me and those who are connected to me, but if it hadn't been for God being on my side, I wouldn't be here today to tell my readers my story. In my book title, *How I Made It Over*, you will see my family's life as we experience some tough times together and how we overcame it together, along with our walk with Jesus Christ.

The Journey Begins

My boyfriend had just proposed to me in front of all my coworkers at the post office, where we both worked. I didn't believe he had it in him, but he proved me wrong. My coworkers and other people were so happy for me that day. It was special, and I loved him for that. Oh yes, there were some haters. They want what you have, and I wasn't mad at them. Truth be told, everyone wants that special man or woman to marry, and it was happening for me.

After receiving my engagement ring before Christmas of 1999, I came to believe that this is it, every man who flirted with me was over. The old year was coming to a closure and going into the new year of 2000. The world was upside down; people were thinking the end was coming, and there were no more years or life left when the year 2000 came in. People were buying water, food, and candles like nobody's business. They were saying the lights would go out, and the banks would close so we wouldn't have money to buy food because our jobs wouldn't be able to produce our checks after 1999 was over. All kinds of things were being said about the year 2000, but I remember saying to my family that we were going to church and when the year rang in, my family and I would be in the Lord's house. I went to the church also for the Lord to bless the ring my husband-to-be had given me.

My whole family was in the packed church on New Year's Eve. When the pastor did the altar call, I went down the stairs to get there. We were on the top, looking down from our seats. People were everywhere; there were no more seats left. I gave my life over to God that night. Something was happening to me in this New Year of 2000. Things took a whole different turn in my life. I wanted a ring; I got that. I wanted to stop smoking; I got that. I wanted a husband, and that was well on its way. I wanted a new house; I got that! As I learned how to live for God, understanding how to do that revealed itself to me by God. I went to the beginner's class at New Hope Baptist Church in Jersey City, New Jersey. They taught us what to do when we came to the altar for salvation and what it meant. Step by step, the class taught salvation from the book of Romans 10:9.

The next step was the Scripture on tithing, I didn't understand, but the mother and first lady taught it with grace and love. At first, I was doing it wrong. I was tithing from the net pay rather than the gross pay. The way I see it, I would rather give God what is due to Him willingly, than for Uncle Sam and all the other people to get their share. Still today, I don't know who FICA is!

As I practiced tithing, there had been times I didn't want to go to church because I had robbed God of His tithes. It was something when you knew you had done wrong, yet God still loved you despite your mess. Those sweet words from God made me get up for church services. I have learned that we will make mistakes and even keep doing it, but as you grow in the Word of God, you become aware of your daily repentance. Now is that something we want to keep asking God all the time and not change? No, we're responsible for our actions. There will come a time that you must be accountable for your growth in walking with God. Although it took some time for me to get there, I kept getting up, going to church, and standing on the tithing line without my tithes. It was my place of repentance to God for my action.

If we confess our sins, He is faithful and just to forgive us our sins and to cleanse us from all unrighteousness.

— 1 JOHN 1:9 NKJV

Every time I got up on the tithing line, I was telling the devil, you have no rule over my life or the lives of those connected to me. The crazy things you do will get you to your next step in God in your ministry. How bad do you want God to bring you through? I learned to put my trust in God for all my trials and tribulations.

> **Bring all the tithes into the storehouse, That there may be food in My house, And try Me now in this," Says the LORD of hosts, "If I will not open for you the windows of heaven And pour out for you such blessing. That there *will* not be *room* enough to *receive it.***

— MALACHI 3:10 TITHES NKJV

Now, after understanding a little better about why we tithe and how to tithe, I prayed to God about making me to be a faithful tither in His house. I prayed for a long time and still today, I pray like that. Tithes are to take care of the house of God and to provide for the community a service in God! Amen.

I kept coming to New Hope Baptist Church to learn the Word of God from Pastor Perry. I was ready for my journey to understand salvation in Christ Jesus. The beginner's class each Sunday morning taught us about salvation in God, and I felt like a baby in that class, but well-loved with care. I was able to open up and ask questions I feared asking! But not anymore. When people really love God, they extend their love to show you Christ in their hearts. I felt loved in New Hope Baptist Church, and after I learned that the book of Romans was the road to salvation, my next step in Christ was baptism. I was so scared that day. Moving into the next step in Christ was scary; I didn't know what to expect, but the best part of the unexpected was I got to see how others handled it first. I was very watchful on how to receive the unexpected in the baptism. Now that my life was in God's hand, He spoke to me through all things like the radio, letters of phrases, and through other people. I was happy that I made the choice to follow Christ.

Now the time has come for me and my husband and family to take our journey to the Poconos in Pennsylvania!

THE MOVE to Pennsylvania

I got married to Howard S. Rouse on April 7, 2000 and was ready to take the next step in God's plan for our life. On July 15, 2000, we moved to the Poconos into our first new house. We packed all of our belongings in the moving truck and our car on this day, and the time came for us to say our goodbyes to our old friends on the block of 121 Storms Avenue in Jersey City, New Jersey second-floor apartment. We formed a circle in the middle of the living room floor, and we prayed for God's protection to follow both cars on the journey to the Poconos. My husband took the truck, and I took the car with the kids and the family cat, Princess. I was so excited, feeling like The Jeffersons, "We're Moving on Up."

I must say that although we prayed for safe traveling, I was still afraid. Not of the move, but the drive; I never had driven long distance before! I prayed the whole trip without the kids knowing. Thank you, Jesus, for keeping me and removing the fear that was inside of me. However, the fog in Pennsylvania was wicked. As we approached Pennsylvania, the roads were wet, and it was still raining. With no street-lights, it was very dark, but we took our time and yes, the traffic was backed up. I didn't care; we were going to arrive safe. As we got closer to our new house, we could breathe again. We arrived at our new house at 618 Forrest Drive in Tobyhanna, Pennsylvania. It was the best feeling that any mother or parent could feel, moving from an apartment into your own house! God was so good to us!

The kids set up their rooms. The girls were together in one room, and my son, the lucky one, had his room to himself. Being the only boy gave him more of an upper hand on the girls. Then my husband and I looked at our master bedroom and loved it. With excitement, we put our belong-ings in their respective places and set up the house. The next day, we just wanted to stop and see what Pennsylvania had to offer my family, so we went out driving, not knowing where we were going. We found a place to have breakfast for cheap. The people were very friendly, and the place had a nice family setting. Then we found a place down in Stroudsburg to shop for groceries; however, we were way off the moun-tain. Later, we found a closer place to shop. Then there was another part of the journey that needed to be fulfilled—to find a church.

I remember praying to God, "Now, Lord, You got us up here in these mountains. Now we need to find a church to worship You!" As the kids made friends in the neighborhood, I would venture out looking for a hairdresser. And right around the corner was a beauty salon with a black owner. She overheard me asking one of her customers about the churches around here. I wanted to keep my faith intact. The owner interrupted the conversation and said to me, "Girl, come on back here. I will tell you a church to go to." Her church, Reaching Out for Jesus Christian Center, was on Main Street in East Stroudsburg. We started talking, and I visited her church with her family and mine. Things were looking good for us.

Getting up that morning, ready to find our way around this new place, everyone was ready and looking good to go to church. We got into the car and prayed to God for traveling mercy along with some other requests, the car wouldn't come on. Understanding what was happening in the spiritual realm, I also understood that the devil didn't want us to get to this church, which also made me mad at the devil. My husband tried to get help from our new neighbors. I stayed behind in the car and prayed, "God, you said if we speak those things that aren't as though they are, they shall be given by faith. I said this car will start so we can go to the house of the Lord!"

When I finished that prayer, I heard God say, "Turn the key…" and when I did, the car started up! "Hallelujah! Oh, what joy I had in the Lord because He heard my prayer!"

When my husband returned, he said, "What did you do?"

I said, "I just prayed!"

Well, we were now on our way to church and when we got there, the people were so loving and caring. It felt good. Church was in a theater setting and when the pastor prayed and called out some things, we were asking God to do, I heard requests about drugs. I stood up and went to the altar on my sister Lisa's behalf. When I got up there, they were lining the people up for prayer. As they started to pray, people fell on the floor. Not understanding what kind of church I was in, I rebuked the devil. See, I was a new babe in Christ, and I thought those people were playing with God. But when the Man of God got to me and had one of the ladies lay hands on my heart, which was sister Emily, I spoke to him and said, "I'm standing in the gap for my sister." He prayed, and it felt so strong, I praised God for it being done right then in faith.

When I left the altar, the Man of God said to me, "The Lord said He's doing it for your sister right now." I was so happy to hear that Word from God through the pastor. My sister had been using drugs for so long in her life. I knew that God could do all things, and she could be delivered. Today, she's drug-free. Hallelujah!

As time went on in that year, we would follow Reaching Out for Jesus Christian Center from the theater to their new location in Scotia, Pennsylvania. Evonne and her family had introduced us to our soon-to-be the new church home. I was ever so grateful for her obedience in leading people into God's house. Being new in my salvation from New Hope Baptist Church in Jersey City, I needed to eat at God's table and to walk into the calling of my life. As I kept coming to ROFJCC ministry, the more my family and I would be welcomed with loving arms.

As time passed, just about every Sunday we would be in the house of God. Let me tell you, this pastor was a gem. He was real in everything he taught in service. Although my children weren't so happy leaving Jersey City and their friends, they had met other friends and adjusted to our new surroundings. As time would pass, we became members of the congregation of ROFJCC! It was a happy time in the Lord.

I could remember the pastor placing me on the nurse's team when I joined. At first, he put me on the choir, but I worked on Saturdays, and that was the day they had practice. Then my husband was placed on the Men of Valor team, and they embraced him with brotherly love. The brothers were always ready to assist with helping the mothers on down to the church families. It was an honor to be a part of this great ministry. Pastor taught from the Word of God with grace and mercy. I was on my way in learning my call in Jesus with ROFJCC. When I got to the Poconos, I had already answered the call of evangelism, but I needed to be taught about the call first.

While working in the ministry of nursing, I learned to be a servant to God and His people. It was with great honor to wear my nurse's uniform every Sunday. I didn't mind wearing it every Sunday because truth be told, I didn't like wearing fancy clothes all the time. Yes, I said it... I just wanted to be used by God and be free doing it, and not worrying about how I looked. See, I came to understand that working ministry at ROFJCC was an on-the-job training. Pastor used us all, and I learned to flow with him as he worked in the spiritual realm of God's anointing in the services. And he worked us all! Being new to this kind of calling was intimidating at times, but I had learned to trust in God even more while in the service. We as a team would come together and pray before getting on the floor of the church service every time in unity.

Love was always in the house of God to me, and if there was a misunderstanding anytime with each other, I would pray about it quietly and watch God fix it. Amen.

For me, operating in the back of the seam was for me. It taught me how to see from God's eyes, pray, and release it into God's hand. Pastor would always say not to talk about the person but pray for them because God knew how to deal with each one of us, in His way. Man didn't know how to forgive like God could. It might not be His exact wording, but I understood what He was saying. My journey in ministry began with me and my family coming to church almost every Sunday.

As we came to Sunday services, Pastor would see us getting out of our van and greet us as "The Get Along Family." That was our nickname from him personally. I loved when he would call us as such, it made us feel a part of the congregation every time we came to church. The church had two services, Sunday morning service and Tuesday night service.

Being new to the area at this time in 2000, I wasn't familiar about the roads for night driving, so I hardly made it out for Tuesday nights. I remember one time I did make it out on a Tuesday night service because I prayed all the way there and I enjoyed that I stepped outside of the box that night. There was this young lady by the name of Crystal aka Jumping Jack Flash, who was a member of the church, when service let out, she would run around my car real fast…lol, and I would ask her: "Why are you doing that?" She would reply, "I'm sending angels to cover you as you drive back home." She blessed me that night, and from there on I was no longer afraid to come out for the Tuesday night service. Although she didn't know my fears of driving in the night to come out for service, God laid it on her heart to cover me with His Angels. Me and her became friends after that, because she lived in the same area as I did. However, our friendship would be short lived because Crystal aka Jumping Jack Flash was in a deadly accident.

I would wonder why the members called Crystal, Jumping Jack Flash, and one day in service without fear, she would play her spiritual guitar when the Holy Spirit would hit the services. I mean without fear, she jumped all over the house of God with her spiritual guitar, of course, people would laugh at her, but she knew how to worship God in Spirit and Truth. She was strange, but I was proud to call her my friend because she believed God in her own special way, I was truly blessed by "Jumping Jack Flash."

As time would pass, I began meeting other members in the church house that would play a major part in my ministry. I remember Pastor telling me sister, "Get Along," it's time to walk into your calling as an evangelist/preacher, and he appointed one of the senior members to teach me the art of writing and preparing a sermon. I am now in the class of on-the-job training, as Reverend Coburn would have me over her house for classes. I could remember before our divine appointment how she would tell me about all her degrees in ministry, who would have known that Reverend Coburn was assigned to me, but God.

It was then I began my journey to understanding the art of homiletics, and I took great pride in going to Reverend

Coburn's house to sit under her teachings. It was truly a blessing to have a pastor who knew my calling in God and how to get me started to become a vessel for God's glory. I was well on my way to being used for the work God had put in me to do here on this earth,

"The Spirit of the Lord is upon Me, Because He has anointed Me To preach the gospel to *the* poor; He has sent Me to heal the brokenhearted, To proclaim liberty to *the* captives And recovery of sight to *the* blind, *To* set at liberty those who are oppressed; To proclaim the acceptable year of the LORD."

— **LUKE 4:18-19 NKJV**

As God would have it, I was asked months later to come to Pastor Carter's house of ministry in Jersey City, New Jersey to come and preach a word for his church. When Pastor Carter asked me to be his minister of the hour into his sanctuary, I was excited and afraid at the same time, because this would be my first appointment in God to go forward in God's glory.

My response to Pastor Carter was: "I would be honored, let me get the blessings of my Pastor Dr. Kenneth L. Pearman."

I remember that Tuesday night service when I brought the

request to the Man of God's attention of my invite to go forward and preach. My Pastor looked me in the eye's and told me, "Rouse you are ready, go in God's grace."

His faith in the God in me was a blessing.

It was a great honor to represent my church, Reaching Out for Jesus Christian Center in honor of God and my Pastor. The day came for me to go forward that Sunday of May of 2006, my family was with me along with my nephews. Pastor Carter's church received me and my family with love; then I was taken to his chamber's to be prayed for and to allow me to look over my sermon. This was my first physical step onto a pulpit to bring a word for God's people, and yes, I had butterflies in my stomach. However, it wasn't my first encounter with God, because I had many spiritual sermons and visitations in God, showing me preaching the gospel. It was amazing to see God's handy work in action, and as I walk down to the altar and take a seat in the pulpit, the butterflies got worse, along with fear. That is when I began to pray in my spirit man, calling on God like nobody's business, and God had me to remember my topic, "Help Is on The Way!"

My God, and as I was addressing the church, a great peace came over me. Then my Pastor's teaching and Reverend Coburn took over me, I then looked out into the congregation. I would see my family's faces looking at me with amazement, oh, how much joy that gave me to see my husband, kids, and my nephews witnessing this move of God upon me. I am with tears as I write this chapter of, *How I Made It Over.* It is my ministry to bring God's people into the faith of salvation and to all that is connected to me.

For God so loved the world that He gave His only begotten Son, that whosoever believes in Him should not perish but have everlasting life.

— JOHN 3:16 NKJV

It was a good time in the Lord at Pastor Carter's Church that morning as God had His way. My Scripture came out of the book of, Matthew 6:25 NKJV:

"Therefore I say to you, do not worry about your life, what you will eat or what you will drink; nor about your body, what you will put on. Is not life more than food and the body more than clothing?"

It is when I put my trust in God to take me to the next step in this calling, that He himself has chosen me for. I went to work at the post office in Jersey City, New Jersey, commuting every day from Tobyhanna, Pennsylvania of the Poconos. For twelve years, God has brought me through them highways and byways safely each day to and from work. While they're at work, me and my friends would take our lunch breaks to minister to our coworkers, we would make ourselves available to pray for whoever wanted prayer. Oh, how much joy it was to come to work and get not only my job done, but also God's job done as well. We ran that building in God's glory, me and my Sisters-in-Christ: Valerie, Glenda, Mila, and Freda, just to name a few. We got so much done in thirty minutes on our lunch break, but we didn't stop there, at every break time, we would have Bible study. Even if only one person would show up, Bible study was still powerful, they would come with such joy to be able to share a Scripture, or just to share a testimony on what God has done for them, or just to ask for prayer. We made ourselves available for God's purpose on the journey to winning souls for God's kingdom, and we did make a great impact in the NJBMC, New Jersey Bulk Mail Center. My job had made ways for me to be used by God in everything I went to do, being new in the faith, I was so excited to do the Will of God. It was my pleasure to work for God on my job, a place where there are so many brokenhearted people. To say hello and God bless you to my coworkers was my blessing to see them smile even when they didn't feel like smiling. There have been times when people would seek for me in my work area just to ask for prayer, or to help them make a wise decision in their life, or just a shoulder to cry on. There have been times when my coworkers would just ask to be heard out on whatever it may be that is bothering them. I made myself available to listen or give a word from God if there was one to give. I didn't take it to be that I was replacing God, because I knew better to think highly of myself.

> **"For I say, through the grace given to me, to everyone who is among you, not to think of *himself* more highly than he ought to think; but to think soberly, as God has dealt to each one a measure of faith."**
>
> **— ROMANS 12:3 NKJV**

Although my coworkers would look for me to encourage them in God's Word, they too have been giving the same measure of faith. I knew it wasn't me they were looking for, but the Jesus I serve that lived in me. As my pastor would say to the evangelists of his church, you would be the first God they would ever see as you minister to the lost. Let me also say, my workplace would be clean so that I would be able to minister to anyone who would come over to my area. Thank you to my supervisors who didn't think it robbery to let God use me on the job. I know God has shown them many blessings even to the ones who said, "This is a workplace not a church." My job was the vineyard, because the souls were ready and so was I, to receive my on-the-job training from God. Anytime you are doing God's Will, there comes breakthroughs, favor, and blessings, but it's not always good:

> **"These things I have spoken to you, that in Me you may have peace. In the world you will have tribulation; but be of good cheer, I have overcome the world."**
>
> — JOHN 16:33 NKJV

It was God's Word that kept me balanced; see, it is my sincere desire to please my God, no matter what. Yes, it was hard at times to stay righteous on the job because evil is always around us in the world, but with God's grace we can do all things in Him, I choose to live for God. "Did I always do good all of the time?" I must tell the truth, I did NOT, but I can admit that to myself and to my Savior. Life will throw you many curveballs, just do not stop catching them, it cannot rain all the time, the sun must shine.

My Family Grows

My family started to grow; it was my oldest daughter at the age of sixteen who would bless me with my first grandson. By ministering to the world, building. God's kingdom on earth, leading lost souls to God, I didn't see the signs of me becoming a grandmother.

I remember how I found out that my daughter was pregnant, it was a Tuesday night in service. Pastor was praying for the people and when it was me and my husband's time to receive prayer, Pastor stopped and said, "Somebody is pregnant, and this baby must come forth."

I looked at my husband and said, "You know it is not me."

We laugh to each other because my husband wasn't having that. One was enough for him. We joked so much that night on the way home, but lo and behold, God spoke to me in my travels to work one day and He showed me a baby boy.

In this vision, I saw a baby boy sitting on the floor, it was in a white setting as if it were God's glory, and he was beautiful. I remember this open vision as if it were yesterday. I said, "Lord, whose baby is this in my subconscious?" And the reply from God was, "This child must be born."

In shock, I could not say anything because I didn't see

where this baby boy was coming from. As time went on, me and my husband was trying to get my baby brother's kids to live with us here in the Poconos. My nephew's mother was having some hard times, and she asked me if I could help her with my nephews, and of course, I would say yes. I was raised to always help my family; it is just in my blood to do so.

For me and my husband to care for my nephews, we had to do some research on children services. The first step was to get fingerprinted, so we went to the police station to have that process done, while waiting, I heard a voice said, "Take one of the pamphlets."

Now, remind you, when I looked at this pamphlet, it was a young girl, she was sad and crying and the caption said, "Are you scared? Are you pregnant? We can help." It was by the guidance of God that led me to a place of understanding His voice.

"My sheep hear My voice, and I know them, and they follow Me."

— JOHN 10:27 NKJV 2

It was the Word of God that ordered my footsteps, I relied on Him to show me how to hear His voice and to obey His commands. And He did, when I got home, I didn't say anything, I handed my daughter the booklet and walked away; waiting for her to come running in the living room yelling, "Mom not me!" However, that wasn't the case, she ran in to the bathroom, I called out her name, and she looked at me with puppy eyes and said yes.

I am so glad I have a relationship with God because my reaction was in Him to be calm. Although I did question Him: *Why my teenage child, Lord?* Then I had to remember the prayer line He gave me called, **Love Peace and Harmony.** See, although I was doing God's Will by praying for others, God was covering my house whole. However, as a servant for God; know that you will be the first partaker of the ministry He called you into. Not knowing that, I learned as I walked with God daily that I am to be the sheep for slaughter for His will.

"Yet for Your sake we are killed all day long; We are accounted as sheep for the slaughter."

— PSALM 44:22 NKJV

Therefore, my family would be my ministry to God, as my walk in God began, so did my ministry with my family. My teenage daughter is pregnant and there is no room for me to be angry. I had to treat her as if it were someone else's child and pray for her to get through this rough part of her life and to encourage her that it is not the end of the world. I know by me accepting the fact that she is about to be a teenage mother, gave her a big relief.

Thanks be to God all hands were on deck, we all had to continue doing our daily duty, the kids going to school, and me and my husband commuting to work. There was no way the devil was going to stop me from working in God's vineyard for souls. So, nine months later, my first grandchild was born and what a blessing he was to be born. My husband was the first one he saw and smiled at. Now this beautiful baby is in all our lives and we cannot stop holding him; the poor baby never could sleep in peace without one of us breathing on him.

My daughter was able to finish her high school studies and graduate with the support of her family, when they say, "it takes a village to raise our children" that is true. My ministry with my daughter begins, now my first grandson is here, and the family is very much overprotective of this great addition to our family.

Still, everyone has a job to complete, going to school was a must in my house, no matter what!

I remember one of the members was opening her own in-house daycare. What a blessing that was and they were close by, it was God's hand in everything concerning my family's safety and obligations to go to school. As well as for me and my husband to continue to commute to work knowing that everyone was being taken care of. It made things easy for us, but we still had some worries being so far away from home. Therefore, it is so important to belong to a good church, so that you could be of service to each other. To this day, I love this member and her family so much, they have blessed me and my family in many ways and in return, God has kept them safe in His arms.

As time would continue, my daughter is graduating from high school and her firstborn son is walking and talking. She is well on her way to being a mother full-time to my grandson and working to make ends meet for the household.

"You shall teach them diligently to your children and shall talk of them when you sit in your house, when you walk by the way, when you lie down, and when you rise up."

— DEUTERONOMY 6:7 NKJV

My first grandson is growing, and he loves to praise God with me, he would mimic me, giving God the praise. It makes me smile all the time to see this little body giving God glory.

"Therefore, whoever humbles himself as this little child is the greatest in the kingdom of heaven."

— **MATTHEW 18:4 NKJV**

When you read God's Word, you will begin to live like the Word tells us. As I would walk in God's path, He would give me on-the-job training with real life issues. If not in my life then in others, I would meet. I found that my walk in God comes with a price, my prayer life would become stronger every time I would pray to God. It is a personal relationship/encounter with God as I grow into my calling.

My Grandkids and Their Nicknames...

How they got their nicknames, each one has a story that comes with their name. My first grandchild got his nickname from one of my best friends, Freda's grandson, she would call her grandson, Grannie-boy... I thought that was the cutest name ever. Freda, God-fearing woman in so many ways, has helped me in my walk with Jesus.

One of my postal buddies at work would join us at the Bible study we would have at lunch break. My friend showed so much love to her grandson, you could see that her love for him was genuine. The way her eyes would receive him when he came into her presence. It was her Grannie-boy at the age of five who prophesied that I was going to be a grand-mother...yes, he did, one day while walking on Jackson Avenue on a summer day in Jersey City, New Jersey.

Grannie-boy called me grandma, and I responded, "Oh no, baby, I'm not a grandmother yet."

Little did I know he was talking right, as you have heard early on in my book about my daughter's teenage pregnancy and how it did come to pass that I was becoming a grandmother.

"And it shall come to pass in the last days, says God, That I will pour out My Spirit on all flesh; Your sons and your daughters shall prophesy, Your young men shall see visions, Your old men shall dream dreams."

— ACTS 2:17 NKJV

As life would have it, I became a grandmother, and my best friend let me adopt her Grannie-boy's nickname for my own grandson's name. My friend, Freda's Grannie-boy is a young man today and he is growing in faith with his grandmother.

My second grandchild got her nickname from her other grandmother, Shu-Shu we call her. Because growing up she was a firecracker, Shu-Shu is that kid who would tell you family comes first and didn't have a problem letting you know at a young age. Although, Grannie-boy is the oldest, his sister was the protector. Yes, you heard right, she was the one for family, you weren't doing anything to her brother if she could help it. I must say, she got it honestly from her Nana/Mother.

In each one of my grandkids you will find a part of me in them all. It is my God-given duty to place what God has given me into them all, so they too would have a God experience in their life as they grow up.

"Train up a child in the way he should go, And when he is old he will not depart from it."

— PROVERBS 22:6 NKJV

God will have us to share what He has poured into us, so that we may help someone else along the way. Given out impartation, so that they too can have that God-given experience in each one of my grandkids, as I watch them grow up, I can see God's work in their life.

My third grandchild's nickname is Red, well she was a stubborn pregnancy because she wanted to come out early. After so many attempts to stop her from coming early, she refused not to, therefore she had to be driven to Lehigh Valley Hospital for her to be delivered. However, she was born bright light with sandy red hair, she hit both sides of her grandparent's white ancestors.

Red was like her mother; they both had that stare as if they could look through you; and never saying a word much as a baby. Her hands were so pretty growing up, I called her hands healing hands.

"By stretching out Your hand to heal, and that signs and wonders may be done through the name of Your holy Servant Jesus."

I have learned to speak into existing the gifts of each one of my grandkids as they were born early in their life, by the grace of God that was given unto me. God has always been my guidance throughout my life; ups and downs, I could always find help from God in times of trouble.

My fourth grandchild's nickname is, Nazzie Wizzie, he enters this world quiet, although there were many distractions heading his way. My daughter had him while going through postnatal distress because nine months after Red was born, here comes baby Nazzie, we called them both Siamese twins. Already a mother of three children, the fourth baby had a hard time getting attention; therefore, Nazzie's Godmother stepped in and cared for him until my daughter was able to do so on her own.

What a blessing it is to have resources in your church home to cover your loved ones when needed. Thank you to Emily Mcilwaine for standing in the gap and still is onto this day.

"Now may He who supplies seed to the sower, and bread for food, supply and multiply the seed you have sown and increase the fruits of your righteousness."

— 2 CORINTHIANS 9:10 NKJV

My fifth grandchild, the baby out of all his siblings, had many nicknames from me, but the one that stuck with him was Buddy. See, Buddy was born with a hole in his heart, and at three months he had his first surgery. But before he would go under the next day, I took Buddy to a Tuesday night service with me, and I remember my pastor giving him back to the Lord for me that night. And sealing him in prayer for his surgery on that next day, what peace I had for my Buddy when I left service that night. To know that God will be with him in the operating room for those nine or ten hours gave me peace to relax while at work. Buddy made it safely through his first surgery that Wednesday morning of January 2012. However, he would need to have another one a few years later to replace the outgrown valve at age seven. Nevertheless, Buddy come through his second heart surgery when he reached seven years old with the grace of God on his side.

Now getting ready to turn nine years old this October sixteenth of the year 2020, my Buddy is strong and continually active in all areas of his growth. Although, he may need another heart surgery when he gets older because he would have outgrown his pervious heart valves. Therefore, we will trust God for His omnipotent healing over my Buddy's life.

"Trust in the LORD with all your heart, And lean not on your own understanding..."

— **PROVERBS 3:5 NKJV**

My sixth grandchild is my son's firstborn and how she got her nickname when she was born, her father was there to welcome her into the world. He was so excited his baby was here, the nurses had assisted him in cutting her umbilical cord before her mother was able to hold her. Long before she was coming, my son kept coming out to tell me to come on in mom... Lord knows I didn't want to see no blood or nothing, that's why with all my grands I waited until they was cleaned up, then I would go in the room to hold them and seal them in God's prayer.

To see my son holding his baby was a blessing to me, I believe that all men should witness the birth of their children out of respect to the mother who carries this life for nine months. So that in return they would be grateful of the mother that will raise their child to be the best they could be. Well, as I held her in my arms, I just could not believe how long this baby was so as she grows. Her nickname became my Giraffe.

I do not know why I was so surprised because my son and the baby's mother are both six feet tall plus. My son was there at all his children's birth, and I admired him for that responsibility as a father to all his kids.

When your own children begin to show the teachings that you have demonstrated to them as they grow into parenthood, it gives you reassurance that they too would be a good parent to their own children. However, there will be some hiccups along the way where they might not do so well as parents, yet they still will have their parents to fall back on for guidance.

"I will instruct you and teach you in the way you should go; I will guide you with My eye."

— PSALM 32:8 NKJV

Did I do good always as a parent myself? No, but I knew who I could turn to for guidance when I fell short in doing so. It makes a difference when you know where all your help comes from in this walk called life journeys.

"I will lift up my eyes to the hills-- From whence comes my help? My help comes from the LORD, Who made heaven and earth."

— PSALM 121:2 NKJV

My seventh grandchild got his nickname later down the road because I wasn't around him as much, but as he got older, he became Juju. Yes, his mother is Puerto Rican / Italian. Now Juju is a split image of his father, growing up huge for his age. His name just came naturally from his birth name, Julius.

With him I can see the fight he has to do things early for himself. My eighth grandchild same mother, Alijah, he is my son's youngest baby, well he was quiet as a baby and still is today. His father nicknamed him, Jah which is fitting for him because my son's father is a Rastafari native of Barbados West Indies. Alijah is my son's youngest baby, when I look at him, I see my son, he is laid back, calm, and he just looks at you and observe who you are. Although, when he sees me coming, he runs…Laugh out Loud!

Later, after watching Juju give me some love, he warms up to me, but his father must be by his side. He is still attached to his mother's umbilical cord as Jah gets older, he would draw near to his Nana, I can wait. In the meanwhile, they know who Nana is, I am good with waiting to connect with them on a one on one level.

"For we through the Spirit eagerly wait for the hope of righteousness by faith."

— GALATIANS 5:5 NKJV

My ninth grandchild got his nickname as soon as he was

born, Buster came into this world with his hands ready to fight, my youngest daughter's firstborn. What can I say about Buster? He is that one who is smart before his time, the things he would say would make you think that you are talking with a mature adult.

When he was a small baby at three months old, I could remember him being in my room, where he always was; and I would get to praising God yelling, "Hallelujah!" This baby would throw his head back and his arms up in the air and join me in praises. You know I was blessed to see him praise God with me even as he got older, today at age four till this day when I pray, my Buster is always in agreement with me with his Amen.

Now, with his sister on the way, making her my tenth grandchild in November of 2020 this year, he is so excited to be a big brother always talking to his mother's belly, singing to his sister and telling her his made-up stories.

I thank God for all my grandkids, they are the reason why this book, *How I Made It Over* is going to be a blessing for so many readers, because without family experience, who can we leave a legacy to?

So that the torch keep moving from generations to come.

My family is my ministry, they are the second imparta-tion for God's glory to rest in them, with me being the first impartation from God, God saved me so that I could be that example for them and for others on the road to salvation.

When I gave my life to the Lord, I answer the called to evangelize God's message to the world; it was a strong will in my spirit to carry out God's Word to the lost and the broken-hearted. What a joy I had to talk with people about the love of Jesus Christ.

When I first got saved, you could not stop me from witnessing God's love. One of my strongest anointings from God is my love spirit in Jesus, just to be able to get people to open up and to receive God's love alone made a major difference in my life and in their life also. When you get saved there's a power that you receive from God that is so unexplainable until you walk in it, you feel invincible, nothing can stop you from believing God's work in your life. Fear never crosses your mind because you know that God can do anything.

"Behold, I send the Promise of My Father upon you, but tarry in the city of Jerusalem until you are endured with power from on high."

— LUKE 24:49 NKJV

Stay under the ministry that God place you with until you have received everything from the Man or Woman of God as you get equipped to do God's work in this world. There will be times when you do not feel that connection with God, as life hit you from every corner of your walk. But always remember God did say,

> **"These things I have spoken unto you, that in Me you may have peace. In the world you will have tribulation; but be of good cheer, I have overcome the world."**
>
> **— JOHN 16:33 NKJV**

The Day I Lost My Mother

On that cold and rainy day, on November 27, 2013, I was planning to go and pick up my mother from work. We were planning this week of Thanksgiving to venture out to Jersey City to get my brother. It was an exciting day for my mother, because she was happy to be getting out of the house to travel. I was excited when I was getting off work that cold and rainy day. At one point I was going to change my mind from the travel, because of the weather. But I knew my brother was waiting patiently for us to come for him.

By the time I was leaving work, I got to my car and looked at my phone before driving off to pick up my mother. In doing so, there I would see a lot of missed calls on my phone from my mother.

Of course, I was like: ***What now?***

My mother was dealing with a lot of illness with her health at the time. So, receiving a lot of missed calls from my mother was at times, scary. As I returned the calls, there would be no answer from her phone. Then I would listen to the messages, to my hearing from the home health aide on the other end telling me she was at the hospital with my mother.

So now I am off from work, ready to take this ride down

to Jersey City, to pick up my brother for our festivity. It was always our family celebrations on the holidays that made my mother so happy. So, to get a message saying she was in the hospital just hurt me so much.

As I was making my way down to the hospital, all I could do was pray, with all that cold rain falling and turning into ice. Now I must drive slow because of the cold rain turning into ice. I wanted to get to my mother fast, but the weather was against me. It was just a day I would never forget, we looked forward to eating together on this Thanksgiving Day. My mother was well-known for her famous stuffing on Thanksgiving Day, no one could touch how my mother made her stuffing from scratch.

So, as I am driving to the hospital, I could see that our trip will not be happening. My brother would be disappointed, but things happen in our life that we just cannot control. So, I get to the hospital to see my mother in much pain because she had fallen in her bathroom at home. She could talk and all, they had given her some pain reliever to relieve her back pain. They had her so heavily sedated, but she knew I was there for her.

When she saw me, her first words to me were, "Baby, I know you are so tired of seeing me in the hospital."

My response was, "No, mommy. It's okay."

But deep down in my heart, I wanted my mother to be healthy again. I knew that she was far from being healthy, because of all her health issues. My mother was suffering in her body, she had to be on oxygen for twenty-four hours a day, right along with high blood pressure and sugar diabetes. Taking medication and going to doctor's appointments was our daily routines. But my mother stays in good spirits always, just for me and her being in each other's company made her happy. Being her oldest daughter made me take on my mother's life decisions.

They had to admit my mother on that cold and rainy November day of 2013 on that 27th day. We could not pick up my brother that Thanksgiving year, but we did celebrate Thanksgiving with my mother on that day. I took the responsibility to be the one to make my mother's famous stuffing, and I must say, I did get her approval as she was eating it that day. How proud I felt that Thanksgiving Day, as we ate together with my mother in the hospital room.

Then the time came that we had to say good night to each other and that we must leave now. "But I will see you tomorrow mommy." The look on her face was the saddest moment for me. Who would have known that we would never have another Thanksgiving dinner together ever again?

My mother lived for the rest of the mouth of November 2013, but on December 2, 2013 my mother transitioned. On that day, sitting next to my mother's bedside holding her hand, I didn't think I was saying goodbye, but my mother could not respond, because she wasn't breathing on her own.

It took some time, but I held her hand until God came to take her home to her big mansion in Heaven.

I mean she was in there from a fall. If I could hear her voice just once to speak with me. You know when you are the caretaker of a loved one, you can get overwhelmed with just the little details of their health issues. My mother was always on point with her medication, she knew every name on those pills. And to see that she could not talk because she was on a machine that was breathing for her, I just didn't believe she was exiting this side of life. But as I remember when I came into her room, I did notice they had markings on my mother's foot. This was alarming to me and I asked, "Why is there an X on my mother's foot?" The nurse responds, "It is the place where we check for her pulse."

I was so out of it that day. All I could do was sit with my mother and hold her hand, I had no more fight in me to argue that issue. As time went by, I called my pastor to ask him to pray for my mother. "She is in the hospital."

He asked me, "Is she talking?"

I said, "No."

My pastor replied to me, "Rouse, I will come there to be with you and your family."

Before he got there, my mother had transitioned into eternity. That was the day I lost the woman who gave me life, my heart was in disbelief to believe that she was gone. The reality was that I now must prepare my mother's homegoing, one of the hardest things I ever had to do, I hadn't one clue on what comes next.

Thank God for all the training I received from my Bishop Kenneth L. Pearman of, Reaching Out for Jesus Christian Center Ministry. By being in place for members in my church who had gone on to be with the Lord, had prepared me to create my own mother's program.

"Let not your heart be troubled; you believe in God, believe also in Me. 2. In My Father's house are many mansions; if it *were* not *so*, I would have told you, I go to prepare a place for you. 3. And if I go and prepare a place for you, I will come again and receive you to Myself; that where I am, *there* you may be also. 4. And where I go you know, and the way you know."

— JOHN 16:33 NKJV

I take comfort knowing that my beloved mother is now resting in the arms of our Lord and Savior. However, for me to get to this point was an extremely hard pill to swallow as I seek peace in my heart for an exceedingly long time, to come to terms that I will not see my mother here on earth anymore. Seven years later, I am telling my story.

Although I had many turns in my life as I journey down this road to, *How I Made It Over*, and yet I am still standing.

My life with my family is the one thing God gave me, to lead them into their destiny, and when they come to that road of which way should I go? They would remember…How Did I Make It Over?

"With Jesus on our side."

"So they said, "Believe on the Lord Jesus Christ, and you will be saved, you and your household."

— ACTS 16:31 NKJV

My Personal Prayer Life

My prayer life has been the biggest part of my walk in the Lord, without having a prayer life, you cannot reach your faith in God.

"Now faith is the substance of things hoped for, the evidence of things not seen."

— HEBREWS 11:1 NKJV

It was in my prayers I put my hope in God, trusting Him to answer them as I kept seeking and believing that He will hear me. When I prayed some time, I would think that I wasn't praying, but all the while, I was simply praying prayers like, **(Lord have mercy on me!)** This was my personal prayer to God every time I would fall short of His glory. We know when we have fallen short with God, but we so often want the Man of God/Woman to tell us our shortcomings. Truth is, we do not need for the preacher to call out our sins, because when you know God for yourself, you then know who you are and who you are in Christ Jesus. I fear God; and this is the wisdom of being so as Scripture states.

**"The fear of the LORD is the beginning of wisdom,
And the knowledge of the Holy One is understanding."**

— PROVERBS 9:10 NKJV

As I look over my life, I could see where God has done it just for me. By keeping prayer open in our life, causes change to take place in us and for our families. Yet, God is still with me, not because I deserve it, no, but because of the Blood of Jesus: God provides for me! Hallelujah. On my journey with God, I found myself still trusting Him and understanding His will for me. My vow to God when I got saved was,

Surely goodness and mercy shall follow me All the days of my life; "And I (Pam) will *dwell in the house of the LORD Forever."

— PSALM 23:6 NKJV

No matter what it looks like in my life, I shall not separate from the love of Christ! God is my rock and I will stand upon It. Amen. But God, He still has His hands on my life, without Him I could do nothing, but with Him I could do all things through Christ who strengthens me on this journey of grace and mercies.

You may ask yourself, all that I have been through why would I keep praising God?

Truth be told, I never stop praising God, but I did stop opening my mouth to share His love when I lost my mother. My heart wouldn't let go of God's unchanging hands within my soul. However, in my pain for so many years, I found it hard to share His Word, because I was angry with God. Yes, I said it.

I must tell my truth in where I was at that point of my life. When my mother transitioned from earth to God's Kingdom, it took me by surprise, I thought my mother would be here to see this book come to pass.

I thank God for my bishop who keeps it real when life's tough experiences come our way while walking with God, it's in your by and by when you realize God is still with you.

How I Made It Over?

Through prayer, praise, and worshipping God!

That is how, because if it hadn't been for God on my side, where would I be? I will tell you where, dead sleeping in my grave! Having a prayer life with God sustained me through my trials and tribulations. There have been times I didn't feel like praying, but God always has a ram in the bush for those who believe in Christ Jesus.

There will come a time in your salvations when problems will overtake you; and you will find yourself not praying. It is not that you do not love the Lord, because the truth is, you love the Lord with all your heart if you know Him as your Lord and Savior.

Sometimes, life happens, and you just feel disconnected from God.

Lord have mercy on me, forgive me Jesus for not opening my mouth to pray, but please hear my heart prayers when my mouth will not open in Jesus' name, I pray. Amen.

There are times where I just had to cry; I remember one time my daughter the oldest one, got herself caught up in some bad trouble with the law. It was my routine to make a stop at my daughter's house to see and kiss on my grandkids after I would get off work from Jersey City, before I would go home.

One day on my visit to her house, I found my nephew there with the kids, so I asked my nephew, "Where is my daughter?"

He gave me a look like Aunt Pam, I do not know.

So, I go outside to question the neighbors, and finally I got word that my child was in jail. My mind could not wrap around the fact that this child of mine was locked up with three small kids at home waiting on her. It was at that very moment, sitting in her living room looking at my grandkids, I started to cry out loud.

My heart was hurting because I was like: *What am I going to do?* I must go to work, and so does my husband and the other two of my children must go to school. I was so through with my daughter; it was at that moment I began to pray in my subconscious.

Lord, I am tired of going through with my daughter, please help me.

When I finished that prayer, my Grannie-boy walked up to me and held my hand and said to me, "Nana, I'm praying for my mommy."

I looked at this young child in his eyes and I was able to connect with his faith in God for his mother's release. I started to pray, and I said.

Lord if this baby could believe You for his mother's deliverance, then so can I.

Again I say to you that if two of you agree on earth concerning anything that they ask, it will be done for them by My Father in heaven.

— MATTHEW 18:19 NKJV

My Grannie-boy always had my spirit as a baby because he was my first grandchild. I would speak into his young life early, for I knew that he was God's promise child for my daughter. He would be the glue to his mother, father, and his siblings. He is sixteen years old and helps his mother with the family, with small things like cooking for his siblings when his mother is at work. And he loves doing things for his mother, they have a great relationship together and he is open to be there for his momma. My gentle giant is his family's protector, and I love his life so much.

Lord, God I thank You for all my grandkids, I thank You for giving me charge over their life to place in them; all Your words that would cause them to be a blessing to many people, they will come in contact with. Amen

I Am Still Here

When I say, I am still here, know that it is an understatement...

Yes, it is only by the grace of God who has covered me in all areas of my life to walk up right before Him. I give all the glory to my Lord and Savior, for Jesus is worthy to be praised. My heart will forever seek after the Lord's guidance because it is my sincere desire to please Him.

I know, no other help, but my Lord's help when needed. He has created in me to worship Him in spirit and truth. My voice shall make a boast in the Lord because He has made me glad. Although these things have happened in my life, I can honestly say, **I Am Still Here!**

I lost my house, but I am still here.

I was homeless, but I am still here.

My children been in jail, but I am still here.

My marriage at times didn't have any light in the tunnel, but I am still here.

Almost lost my grandkids, but I am still here.

I was in two accidents in two different cars, but I am still here.

I lost my mother, but I am still here.

I almost stop witnessing for God, but I am still here.

My prayer life didn't have life at times, but I am still here.

I had stopped letting God use me for His glory, yet I am still here.

My Savior has kept me in His loving arms, and I am still praising Him. God has made a way out of no way for me and I am still praising Him. The Lord has His hands on my life, and I am still praising Him. I could not stay down on my journey, because my family needs God's anointing in their life too, and I am still praising Him.

Praise the LORD! Praise God in His sanctuary; Praise Him in His mighty firmament!

Praise Him for His mighty acts; Praise Him according to His excellent greatness!

Praise Him with the sound of the trumpet; Praise Him with the lute and harp!

Praise Him with the timbrel and dance; Praise Him with stringed instruments and fluted!

Praise Him with loud cymbals;

Praise Him with clashing cymbals!

— PSALM 150:1-6 NKJV

Hallelujah, Hallelujah, and Hallelujah.
I am still here, and I am still Praising the Lord. Amen.

Thank You

I would like to thank God who is the head of my life and my keeper, throughout my life experiences.

Thank you to my Pastor/Bishop Kenneth L. Pearman for all your prayers and encouragements for the past twenty years for me and my family, you have been a great blessing to us all.

Thank you to The First Lady aka The Duchess, who told me many years ago to not stop coming to church, when I was all alone many times.

Thank you to Shepherdess Natasha Pearman-Pile, who gave me insight on how to write my book and to focus on writing; that the chapters will come later, and it Did!

Thank you to sister Emily Mcilwaine for standing in the gap for my grandkids, and her Godson.

Thank you to Reverend Coburn for being obedient to the assignment giving her from God/Bishop to teach me the art of Homiletics.

Thank you to Sharnel Williams aka Boss Lady of Shar-Shey Publishing, for waiting patiently for my manuscript on this book.

I also want to thank my church family Reaching Out for Jesus Christian Center, for all your love, prayers, encouraging words, and Unity in Oneness together for Our Lord and Savior.

To my whole family, thank you for your good, the bad, and the ugly, because if it have not been for you all; *How I Made It Over* could never become a book of our Testimony. Love You Guys. Amen.

Shar-Shey Publishing Company, LLC

Thank You...

Sharnel Williams CEO

I'm a Wife, Mother, Author, Radio Host, Entrepreneur, Motivational Speaker, and Grandmother. Born and raised in the projects in Newark, NJ, I have two kids, one living and one passed away from leukemia back in 2005, two days after his 12th birthday. I started my own publishing in 2016, called Shar-Shey Publishing Company LLC. I have so much to give to others. I was nominated twice in 2015 and 2016 for my writing, with the Monroe County Image Awards In PA. I have done several speaking engagements. I will continue telling my story to inspire others. I started in 2017, putting together my first "You Are Not Alone" Women Empowerment Luncheon, which will also motivate and inspire people. Now, I'm on my 4th one I love helping others, that's why I do what I do. I'm on a mission to grow my company and turn my first book into a movie I want to thank all my supporters. Don't Give Up On Your DREAMS.

Contact Information

Phone: (973) 348-5067
Email: sspublishingcompany@gmail.com
Website: www.sharsheypublishingcompany.com

sspublishingcompany   Sharnelw

CPSIA information can be obtained
at www.ICGtesting.com
Printed in the USA
LVHW050359080221
678682LV00013B/1006